Congratulations!

Love,

"Grand" GodFather Ray

Fifo Musical Animals ABC

By Hayley Rose

Illustrated by Mark Sean Wilson

Flowered Press

Fifo Musical Animals ABC written by Hayley Rose

Cover design and illustrations by Mark Sean Wilson

ISBN: 0-9982483-0-4

ISBN: 978-0-9982483-0-1

Library of Congress Number: 2016917981

Flowered Press
8776 E. Shea Blvd. #106-213
Scottsdale, AZ 85260

Flowered Press

Printed in China

I dedicate this book to my wonderful girlfriend
Christine Onorati who brings joy to me every day.
~ Mark

To Sydney, my favorite niece, for her love of music.
~ Hayley

Other books by Hayley Rose

Creating fun, educational and inspiring books for kids.

Welcome to the magical world of animals and instruments.
Enjoy the show...

Fifo plays the accordion with an aardvark.

Fifo plays the bongos with a bat.

*F*ifo plays the clarinet with a cat.

Fifo plays the drums with a dog.

Fifo plays the euphonium with an elephant.

*F*ifo plays the flute with a ferret.

Fifo plays the guitar with a giraffe.

Fifo plays the harp with a horse.

Fifo plays the igil with an iguana.

*F*ifo plays the janggu with a jaguar.

*F*ifo plays the keyboard with a kangaroo.

Fifo plays the lusheng with a llama.

Fifo plays the mandolin with a moose.

Fifo plays the nagak with a numbat.

Fifo plays the oboe with an otter.

Fifo plays the piano with a possum.

*F*ifo plays the quena with
a quail.

Fifo plays the repinique with a rat.

*F*ifo plays the saxophone with a sheep.

Fifo plays the tuba with
a tiger.

Fifo plays the ukulele with an uakari.

Fifo plays the violin with a vulture.

Fifo plays the wind chimes with a walrus.

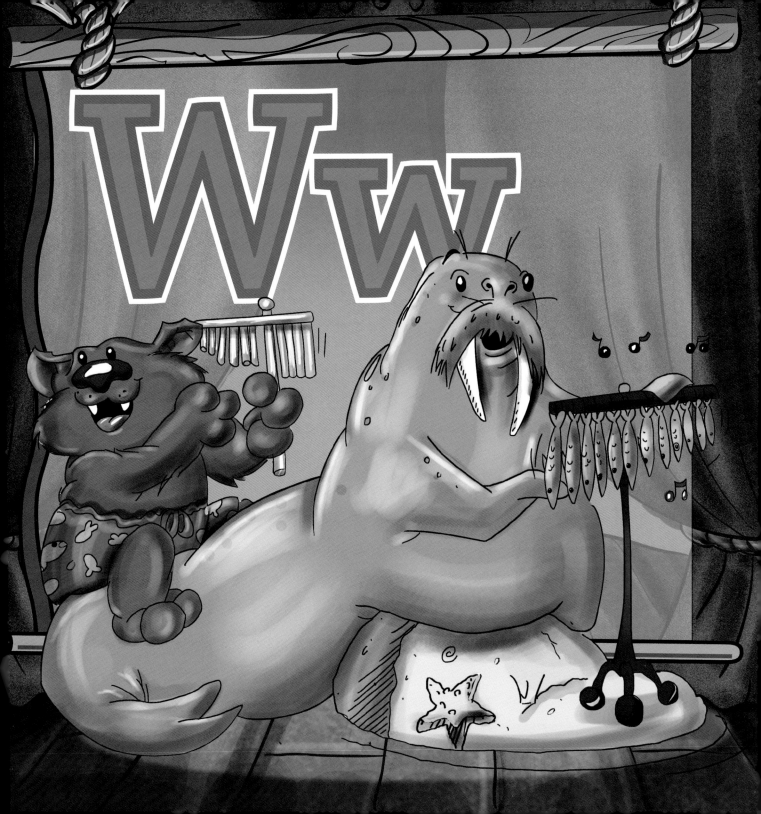

Fifo plays the xun with a xerus.

Fifo plays the yunluo with a yak.

Fifo plays the zither with a zebra.

What is your favorite Instrument?

What is your favorite animal?